This Book Belongs To

Princess: ....

Enjoy bringing these princesses to life with your colors and imagination!

From your magical friend,
Christian Garrett

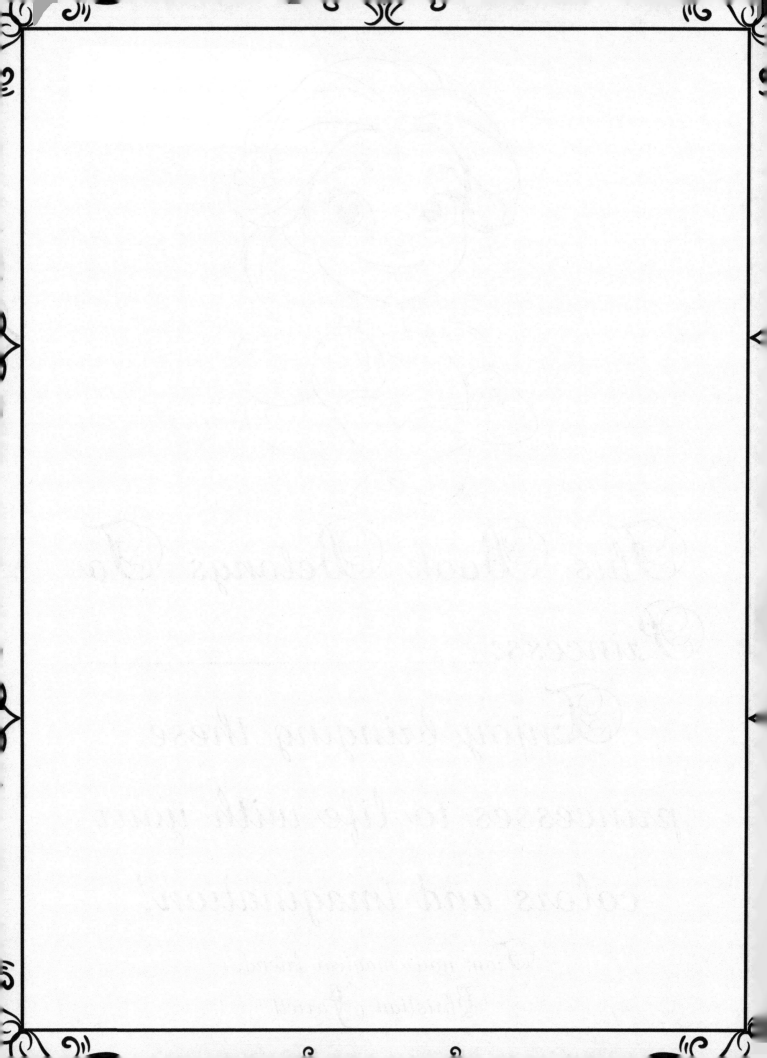

A Fun Gift For Your Kid

Thank you a ton for snagging this awesome coloring book!

As an added bonus, I've got some super fun FREEBIES for your little one to grab and have a blast with.

Instructions:

Open the camera on your phone (as if you're going to take a photo).

Hold the phone over the QR code below.

A link will appear on your screen.

Tap on the link to get your free download!

If you don't see the email in your inbox within a few minutes, please check your spam folder just in case it got lost along the way.

With deep appreciation, Christian Garrett

Every princess has a magical castle. What would your fairy-tale castle look like?

Princesses often have special dresses for magical occasions. What would your princess dress look like?

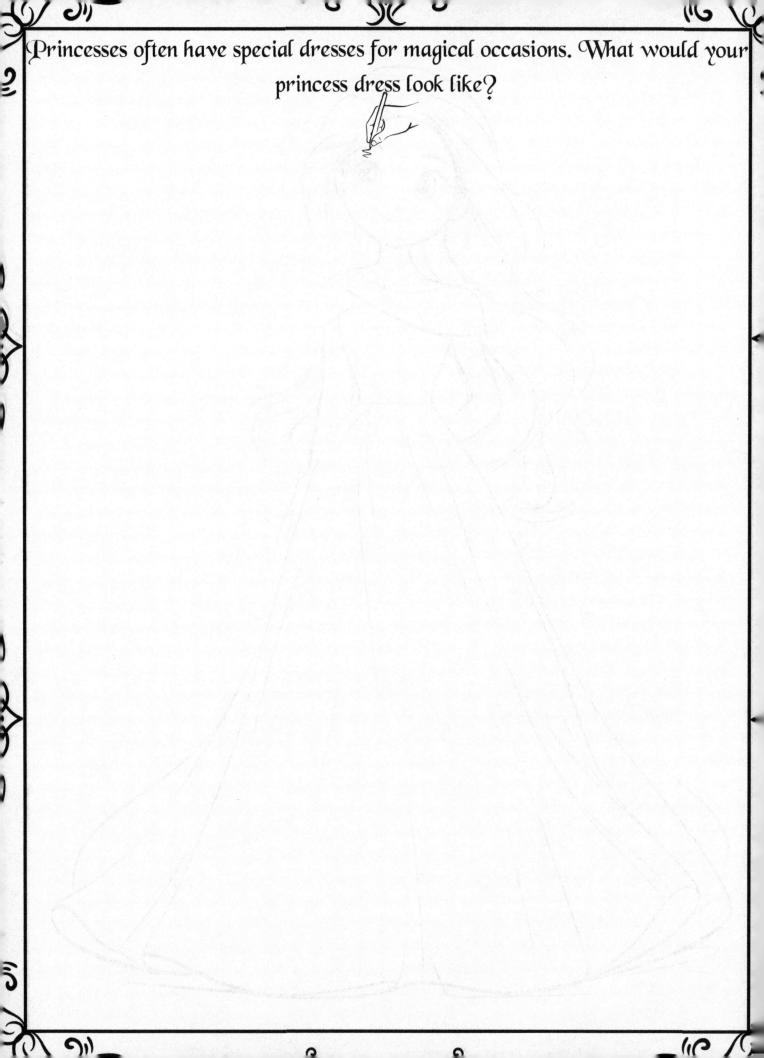

Many princesses have adorable friends: unicorns, dragons, or even talking birds! Draw your magical friend.

Some princesses have special magical powers. What kind of magic would you like to have?

Princesses often decorate their royal rooms with beautiful things. What would your royal room look like?

Every princess has a crown that's unique to her. What would your crown look like?

Princesses sometimes ride magical creatures, like flying horses or giant swans. What magical creature would you ride?

Princesses love to have royal tea parties with their friends. Who would you invite to your royal tea party?

Some princesses live in enchanted forests with talking animals. What kind of talking animals would live in your forest?

A princess's royal garden is full of colorful flowers and butterflies. How would you design your royal garden?

Every princess has a special throne where she sits. What would your royal throne look like?

Princesses sometimes wear magical jewelry that glows with light. What magical jewelry would you wear?

Princesses often have big celebrations with fireworks. How would you design your royal fireworks?

Princesses sometimes have magical wands that sparkle with magic. How would your magic wand look?

Princesses love to explore new lands on exciting adventures. Where would your royal adventure take you?

Every princess has a royal flag that represents her kingdom. What would your royal flag look like?

Some princesses love to sail the seas on royal ships. What would your royal ship look like?

Princesses often have magical shoes that can take them to faraway places.
What kind of magical shoes would you wear?

Every princess has a special treasure chest. What kind of treasure would be inside yours?

Every princess has a special book of spells and stories. What would be inside your magical book?

Princesses sometimes have musical instruments that play beautiful songs.
What instrument would you play?

Some princesses love to fly on magical carpets. Where would your magical carpet take you?

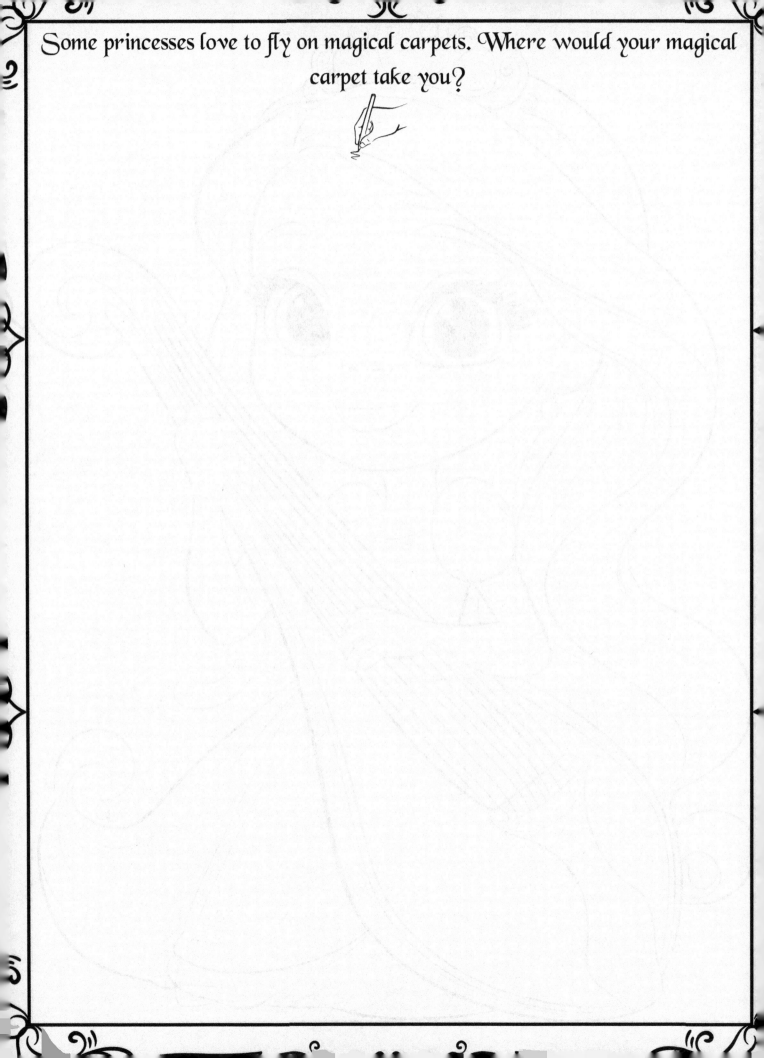

Some princesses can talk to the stars in the night sky. What would the stars say to you?

Some princesses have enchanted mirrors that show amazing things. What would your magical mirror show you?

Princesses sometimes have crowns that change color based on their feelings.
What color would your crown be today?

Every princess has a favorite flower that brings her good luck. What would your lucky flower look like?

Princesses sometimes go on exciting quests to find hidden treasures. What treasure would you search for?

Every princess loves to design her own royal outfit. What would your royal outfit look like?

Princesses sometimes help their kingdoms by building amazing bridges. What would your royal bridge look like?

Every princess has a trusted advisor, like a wise owl or a talking cat. Who would be your royal advisor?

Princesses sometimes travel to faraway lands on magical clouds. What would your flying cloud look like?

Some princesses live in underwater palaces where fish and dolphins are their friends. What would your underwater palace look like?

Some princesses wear special gloves that give them magical abilities. What kind of gloves would you wear?

Princesses often ride through their kingdoms on beautiful horses. What would your royal horse look like?

Some princesses have magical lanterns that can light up the darkest night.
What would your magical lantern look like?

Every princess has a special key that unlocks a secret door. What would your secret door lead to?

Princesses sometimes have magical fountains that grant wishes. What would you wish for?

Some princesses have best friends who are fairies. What would your fairy friend look like?

Princesses often have royal feasts with magical food. What kind of magical food would you serve at your royal feast?

Every princess has a magical library full of ancient books. What kind of book would you find in your library?

Princesses sometimes have talking birds that deliver messages. What message would your bird bring?

Some princesses can turn ordinary objects into gold. What object would you turn into gold?

Some princesses wear shoes that let them walk on clouds. What kind of shoes would you wear to walk on clouds?

Princesses sometimes have magical butterflies that guide them through the forest. What would your butterfly look like?

Princesses sometimes have enchanted shields to protect their kingdoms. What would your magical shield look like?

Every princess has a royal pet, like a kitten, unicorn, or dragon. What would your royal pet be?

Every princess has a royal pet, like a kitten, unicorn, or dragon. What would your royal pet be?

Princesses sometimes make potions with magical ingredients. What kind of potion would you create?

Some princesses can talk to the moon and stars. What secret would the moon tell you?

Thank You!

Dear Friend,

As the author of this coloring book, I want to express my sincere thanks for choosing my book and completing this journey together. It's truly heartwarming to know that my small, family-owned business has been a part of your life.

I pour my heart and soul into creating coloring books that inspire and empower young minds. Knowing that you've found this book to be a source of joy, encouragement, and growth fills me with immense gratitude.

If you enjoyed this coloring book, I'd be incredibly grateful if you could leave a review on Amazon. Your words can make a huge difference for a small business like mine. Your support will not only help me reach more children but also inspire me to continue creating meaningful coloring books.

I know leaving a review might seem small, but it means the world to me. Your support will enable me to keep creating books that touch the lives of young readers and nourish their imaginations.

Thank you again for being part of this journey.

With deep appreciation,
Christian Garrett

Royal Imagination Medal
Congratulations,

You've finished coloring every princess and unlocked the Royal Imagination Medal! Your creativity has made the kingdom even more magical.

Keep dreaming big!

Date:

_____

Christian Garrett

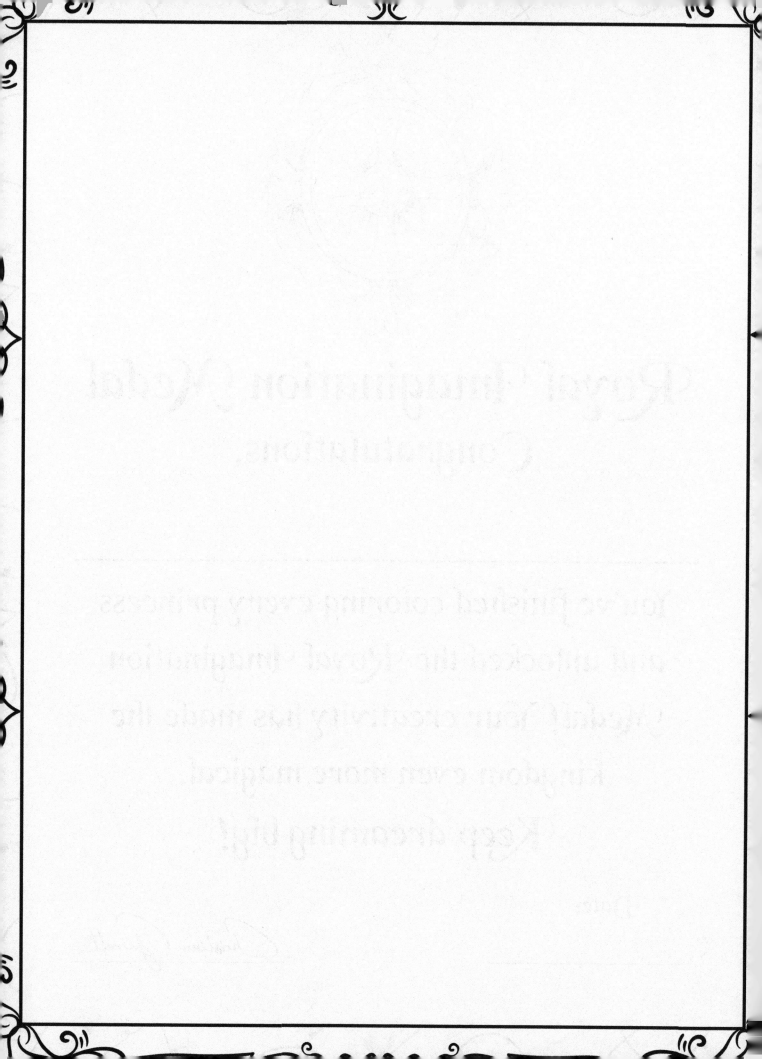

Made in the USA
Columbia, SC
02 January 2025

51063993R00063